For Evan, whose love of fact books ignited my own. And for Emma, who loves myths and stories and shares them with me. KS

For Marlow and Albertine – my mythical creatures. LR

First published by Allen & Unwin in 2024

Copyright © Text, Kate Simpson 2024
Copyright © Illustrations, Leila Rudge 2024

All rights reserved. No part of this book may be reproduced or transmitted in any form or by any means, electronic or mechanical, including photocopying, recording or by any information storage and retrieval system, without prior permission in writing from the publisher. The Australian *Copyright Act 1968* (the Act) allows a maximum of one chapter or ten per cent of this book, whichever is the greater, to be photocopied by any educational institution for its educational purposes provided that the educational institution (or body that administers it) has given a remuneration notice to the Copyright Agency (Australia) under the Act.

Allen & Unwin
Cammeraygal Country
83 Alexander Street
Crows Nest NSW 2065
Australia
Phone: (61 2) 8425 0100
Email: info@allenandunwin.com
Web: www.allenandunwin.com

Allen & Unwin acknowledges the Traditional Owners of the Country on which we live and work. We pay our respects to all Aboriginal and Torres Strait Islander Elders, past and present.

 A catalogue record for this book is available from the National Library of Australia

ISBN 978 1 76118 034 7

For teaching resources, explore allenandunwin.com/learn

Illustration technique: watercolour and coloured pencil

Cover and text design by Kristy Lund-White
Set in 12 pt Halcyon and Pinelopi
Colour reproduction by Splitting Image, Wantirna, Victoria
This book was printed in February 2024 by 1010 Printing Limited, China

10 9 8 7 6 5 4 3 2 1

 The paper in this book is FSC® certified. FSC® promotes environmentally responsible, socially beneficial and economically viable management of the world's forests.

www.katesimpsonbooks.com
www.leilarudge.com

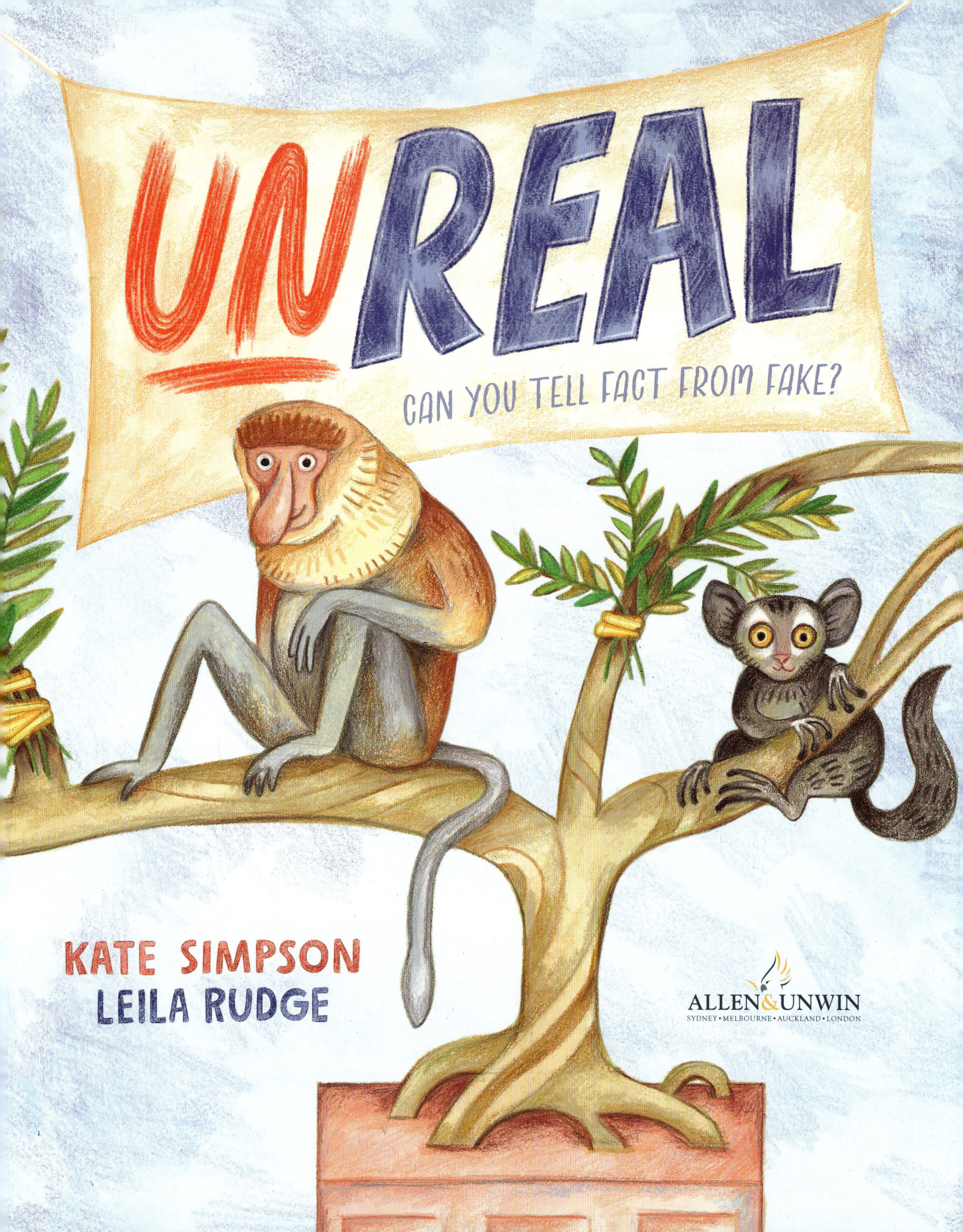

Oh, hello!
What are you doing here?

This exhibit isn't open right now. In fact, I've got a bit of a problem. Some of the displays from our Myths and Legends exhibit were brought here to the Natural History wing by mistake. I don't know how I'm going to fix things. Could you help me sort the real-world animals from the myths?

Real or UNreal?

How can you sort what's real from what's not? It isn't always obvious. As you look at the museum exhibits, you'll be using your gut and logic to help you decide which creatures seem the most likely to be true, but take care! Most people are not as good at telling fact from fiction as they think they are.

Sorting Fact from Fiction

Here are five questions you can ask to decide if information is reliable:

1 **Who is providing me with this information?** Reliable sources can include encyclopaedias, textbooks and the websites of respected organisations.

2 **Do they have evidence for their claims?** Not all evidence is equal. A paw print might be evidence of a new species, but a live specimen would be far more convincing!

3 **Why are they telling me this?** Will someone benefit if I believe this information? Would it make me more likely to buy their product or vote for them in an election?

4 **How recent is the information?** Old information may be out of date, while very new information such as breaking news and the latest scientific discoveries might not have been thoroughly checked yet.

5 **Do other sources agree?** The first source of information you find may not always be the best. Find out what multiple sources say to help you work out whether the information is reliable, debatable or just downright wrong.

CONTENTS

- 6 — Into the Deep
- 10 — Predators
- 14 — Megafauna
- 18 — Life Below Ground
- 22 — Cryptids
- 24 — Bioluminescence
- 28 — Among the Branches
- 32 — Healing Powers
- 36 — A Fish Out of Water
- 40 — Plants and Fungi
- 44 — Hoaxes and Jokesters
- 46 — Animal Mash-ups
- 50 — Extreme Habitats
- 54 — Remarkable Reptiles
- 58 — It Was THIS Big!
- 62 — Conclusion
- 64 — Index

Into the Deep

Oceans cover more than 70% of the Earth's surface, but humans have explored very little of them. Which of these bizarre creatures truly inhabits the deep? Can you find the odd one out?

1 Kraken

Watch out if you're sailing near Norway, Iceland or Greenland! This giant cephalopod is large enough to sink a ship.

2 Vampire squid

What's in a name? *Vampyroteuthis infernalis*, 'the vampire squid from hell', is neither a vampire nor a squid.

3 Marine iguana

Don't be frightened of this gentle giant. It may look monstrous, but it is actually a peaceful herbivore.

4 Narwhal

With a spiral tusk that grows up to 3 metres long, it looks like a cross between a dolphin and a unicorn.

5 Lamprey

Its round mouth sports dozens of hooked teeth that it uses to latch onto its prey while it sucks their blood.

In the Galapagos Islands, home of the **marine iguana**, there is little edible vegetation on land. To stay alive, the iguana has evolved to feed on algae growing on the rocky seafloor. Good manners are not its strong point. While on land, it spends much of its time snorting and sneezing out a concentrated salty liquid that often dries into a white salt crust on its forehead.

REAL

The **narwhal** is a type of whale that lives in the icy waters of the Arctic, feeding on fish, cuttlefish, squid and shrimp. The purpose of its long, spiral tusk is something of a mystery to scientists. The male narwhal is sometimes seen using its tusk to stun prey but the female – which rarely has a tusk – hunts perfectly well without it.

REAL

REAL

The **lamprey** has roamed the seas for hundreds of millions of years, since a time long before dinosaurs. Carnivorous lampreys drink the blood of their prey, latching on using a suction-cup mouth and rows of sharp teeth. But not all lampreys are carnivorous. Some eat nothing at all once they are fully grown, living for months without food before reproducing and then dying.

The **vampire squid** isn't nearly as frightening as its name suggests. It doesn't hunt, instead eating small particles of passing animal and plant matter that it catches on its sticky tentacles. When it feels threatened, the vampire squid can turn itself inside out, showing an underside covered in spines. If that makes you nervous, never fear! It lives hundreds or even thousands of metres below the surface, so your chances of meeting one are pretty much zero.

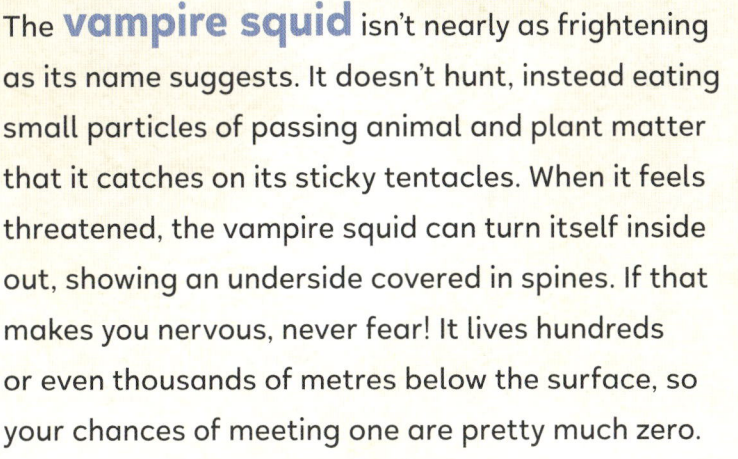

REAL

For hundreds of years, Nordic sailors told stories of a colossal sea monster with an appetite for human flesh. According to legend, a direct attack from the **kraken** was not the only risk to sailors. The gargantuan beast was said to be so large that crews would mistake it for an island and try to land on it. When they did, the kraken would descend, sucking the sailors down with it in an enormous whirlpool.

UNREAL

Fabulous!

We've found our first impostor: the **kraken**. Did it have you fooled? Some myths and legends have a basis in reality, which can make them even harder to spot. The legend of the kraken was probably inspired by the real-life giant squid, which is more than 10 metres long!

9

Predators

Equal parts frightening and fascinating, predators are some of the most exciting members of the animal kingdom.

Wolverine

Tough, ferocious and determined, it will take on animals many times its own size if it needs to.

Chupacabra

This canid is best known for drinking the blood of its prey while leaving the body uneaten.

Tasmanian devil

Today, it's a much-loved Australian icon, but in the 1800s killing one could earn you a reward of 3 shillings and sixpence.

Grey nurse shark

Many animals kill, but few start as young as this shark. In a battle for survival, the pups kill and eat their siblings while still in their mother's womb.

Murder hornet

This startling nickname comes from its habit of tearing the heads off bees and feeding the bodies to its young.

The **grey nurse** is one of the most critically endangered sharks in the world, due in part to its unusual way of breeding. While other shark species commonly give birth to a dozen or more pups at a time, a grey nurse female only gives birth to two: one for each of her wombs. Before birth, the most developed embryo in each womb will devour its siblings until it is the last shark standing.

REAL

REAL

The **Tasmanian devil** was given its name by early European arrivals to Australia, probably due to its eerie growls and screeches. Farmers, who were worried about their chickens, hated the devils and the government offered a reward for each one killed. Since the 1990s, devil populations have been threatened by a fatal illness called devil facial tumour disease. Conservationists are working hard to save the species.

FUN FACT

Baby Tasmanian devils are called imps.

Predator or murderer? You decide. When hunting alone, the **northern giant hornet** typically kills a single bee at a time to feed to its young, but as a group, they are capable of far more damage. In only a few hours, 10 to 50 hornets can destroy a colony of tens of thousands of honey bees, tearing their heads from their bodies and earning the nickname 'murder hornet'.

If you live in the icy northern wilderness of Canada, Alaska, Russia or Northern Europe, it pays to be tough. Only as big as a medium-sized dog, the **wolverine** eats whatever it can find and sometimes brings down caribou many times larger than itself. It can travel dozens of kilometres per day across difficult terrain and through deep, soft snow. And it does almost all of it alone, seeking out other wolverines only in mating season.

The **chupacabra** is an urban legend from Puerto Rico that has spread through Latin America and the southern USA. In early tellings, the chupacabra was described terrifyingly as a kind of reptilian kangaroo, but most people now claim it is a dog-like creature, sometimes with spines down its back. The name chupacabra, or 'goat sucker', comes from its blood-only diet.

Megafauna

The word *megafauna* means 'large animals'. Today's megafauna includes elephants, giraffes, whales, bears and bison. Tens of thousands of years ago, Earth's population of megafauna was much more varied and widespread.

Megalodon

Is this the most terrifying shark that ever lived? This prehistoric sea creature is estimated to have grown to around three times the length of a modern-day great white.

Ground sloths

How big is a sloth? Today, they grow to less than 1 metre long and weigh under 10 kilograms. But their enormous ancestors were around the size of an elephant.

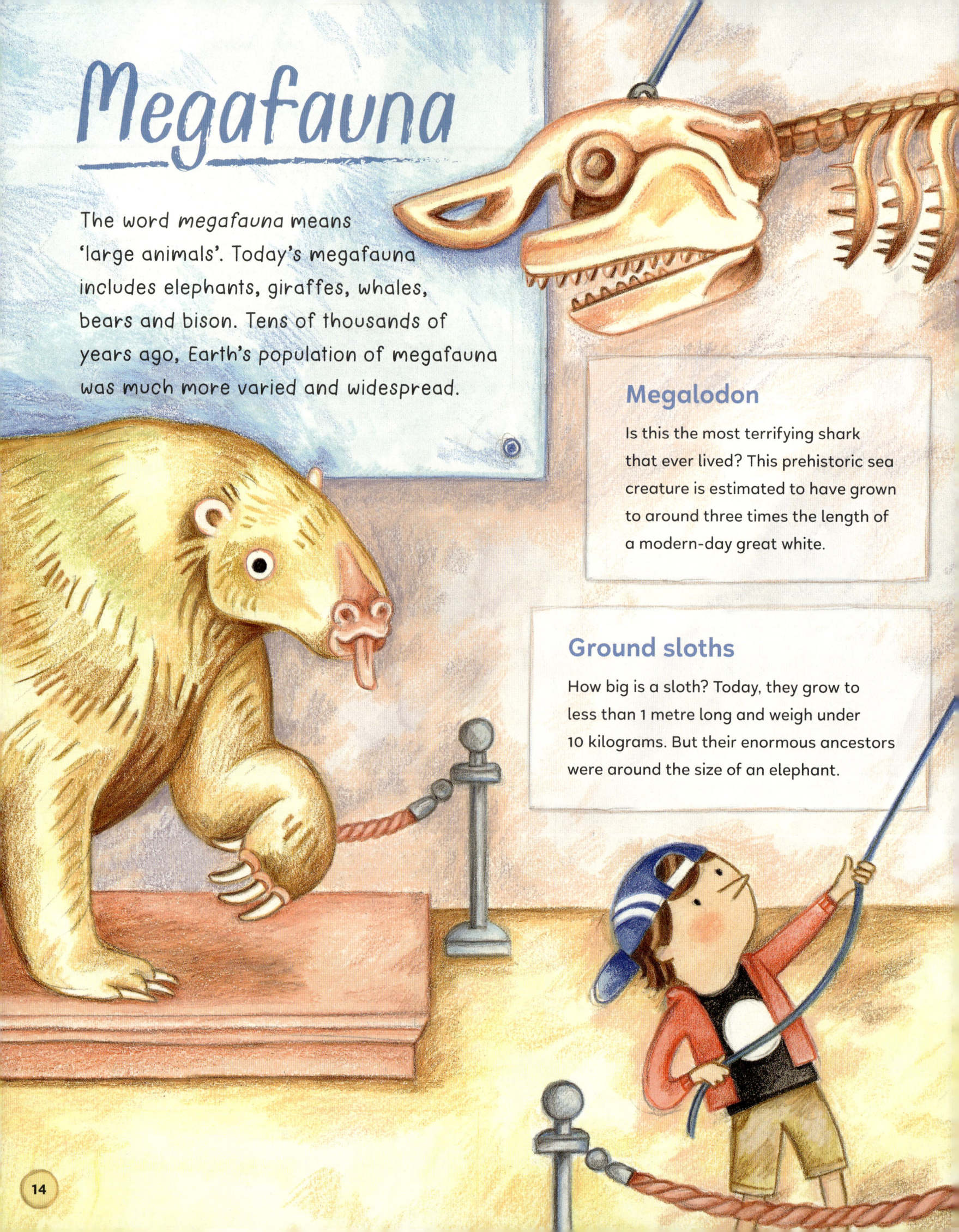

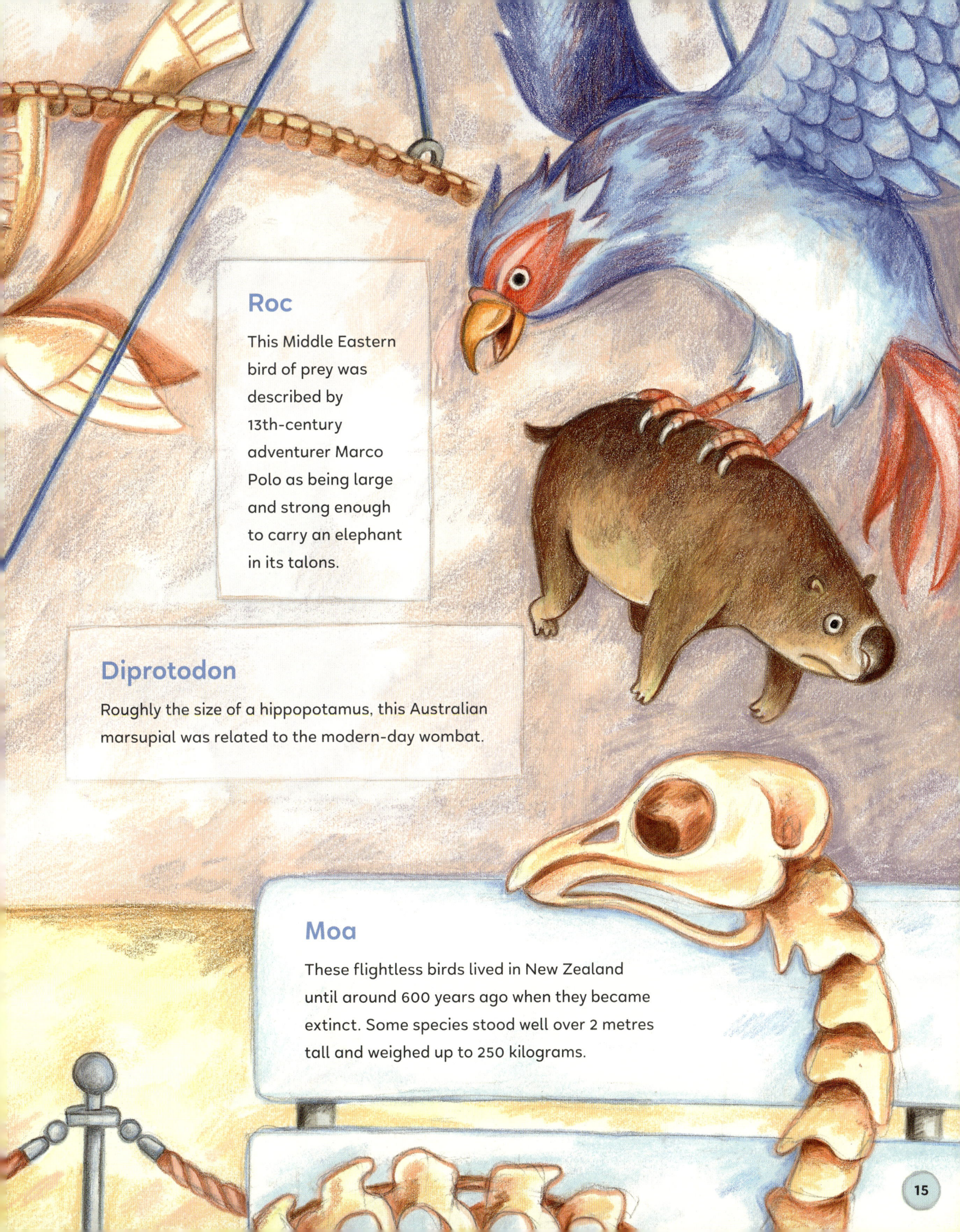

Roc

This Middle Eastern bird of prey was described by 13th-century adventurer Marco Polo as being large and strong enough to carry an elephant in its talons.

Diprotodon

Roughly the size of a hippopotamus, this Australian marsupial was related to the modern-day wombat.

Moa

These flightless birds lived in New Zealand until around 600 years ago when they became extinct. Some species stood well over 2 metres tall and weighed up to 250 kilograms.

Most of what we know about the **megalodon** we have learned from its terrifying teeth. The megalodon's skeleton was made of cartilage, which does not form good fossils, but thousands of fossilised teeth have been found in oceans all over the world. Their enormous size has led scientists to conclude that the megalodon grew to up to 18 metres long with a jaw over 3 metres wide.

Moa were a group of birds ranging from the size of a turkey to giants that were among the largest birds to have ever lived. When the first humans arrived in New Zealand around 1300 CE, the flightless moa, which had previously had no predators, were easy prey for their skilled hunters. Within a few hundred years, the moa were extinct.

UNREAL

The **roc** is a legendary bird of prey from Middle Eastern folklore. It was said to look like an eagle but with a wingspan of more than 20 metres. Its prey included giant snakes that were themselves big enough to eat elephants. Although there is no evidence that the roc ever existed, scientists have found fossils of a prehistoric bird of prey with a wingspan almost twice that of the largest birds alive today.

REAL

The **diprotodon** roamed the inland plains of Australia from around 1 million years ago until its extinction between 25,000 and 45,000 years ago. This giant marsupial, which was as tall as a human and weighed about as much as a modern-day hippopotamus, lived alongside other giants such as an echidna the size of a sheep and a goanna that grew up to 5 metres long.

REAL

The ancient **ground sloths** were not the cute tree-dwellers we know and love today. The largest species weighed up to 4 tonnes and were 3.5 metres tall when standing on their hind legs. Other ancient sloth species took a different evolutionary path, evolving to live much of their lives on the seafloor, swimming and munching on seagrass like a modern-day dugong.

Life Below Ground

We humans are often unaware of what goes on right beneath our feet. These unusual animals live at least part of their lives underground.

Mongolian death worm

Native to the Gobi Desert, this large worm grows to around 60 centimetres long and excretes toxins through its skin. A single touch can be fatal.

Star-nosed mole

Almost completely blind, it uses a star-shaped sensory organ on its snout to 'see' its surroundings.

Naked mole-rat

It's an incredible survivor – resistant to ageing, able to survive in low oxygen environments and impervious to some types of pain.

Turtle frog

While most frogs prefer ponds or other watery environments, this species lives in a sandy burrow up to 1.2 metres deep.

Sydney funnel-web spider

Its venom can kill a human in as little as 15 minutes. Fortunately, a lifesaving antivenom has been available since the 1980s.

The **funnel-web spider** is an ambush hunter that hides in burrows and uses silk trip lines to alert it to passing prey. It then darts out and attacks with a venomous bite. At the Australian Reptile Park, north of Sydney, the venom of hundreds of Sydney funnel-web spiders is milked by staff year-round to help create a life-saving treatment for bites from this otherwise deadly spider.

The **star-nosed mole** boasts one of the most sensitive touch organs in the animal kingdom – a star-shaped arrangement of feelers only around 1 centimetre across but packed with tens of thousands of touch receptors. Because it lives so much of its life underground, sight is of little use to the mole. Instead, its brain creates an image of its surroundings based on touch signals it receives from its snout.

The **turtle frog** – so called because it looks like a small, shell-less turtle – lives in a part of Western Australia where there is little rainfall. Without access to the ponds and pools preferred by many frogs, it uses its strong front legs to burrow more than a metre into the moist, sandy ground, where it feeds on termites. It is one of many frog species whose babies skip the tadpole stage and are born directly as tiny frogs.

REAL

The **naked mole-rat** – small, almost hairless and virtually blind – may not look inspiring, but this unassuming rodent has some impressive adaptations. It doesn't seem to feel pain when exposed to things like acid that would hurt other mammals. It lives in low oxygen environments and can survive up to 18 minutes with no oxygen at all. And to top things off, its lifespan is about five times as long as expected for a rodent its size.

UNREAL

The **Mongolian death worm** is legendary among the peoples of the Gobi Desert in Central Asia. It has been described as poisonous to the touch and able to spit acid and discharge electricity at its prey. Although the death worm has never been shown scientifically to exist, these frightening behaviours are all found elsewhere in the animal kingdom.

Cryptids

A cryptid is an animal that some people believe is real but whose existence isn't backed up by strong evidence.

Loch Ness monster

Lake monsters of various types exist in legends all over the world, but none is as famous as Scotland's Loch Ness monster. Since the first sightings of Nessie in 1933, there have been many attempts to find solid evidence of her existence, including exploration with submarines and sampling of the loch floor in search of bones. None have been successful, but that doesn't stop the hundreds of thousands of people who visit the loch each year from staring out at the water, hoping for a glimpse.

Bigfoot

Bigfoot – also called the sasquatch – is a legendary ape-like creature that captured the imagination of North Americans in the 1950s. Most of the 'evidence' of Bigfoot comes in the form of enormous footprints, but in 1967 two filmmakers recorded footage of a creature they claimed to be Bigfoot. Over 50 years later, believers and sceptics remain divided over whether the footage genuinely shows the sasquatch of legend or just a person in a gorilla suit.

Could cryptids exist?

Scientists estimate that around 80% of all species have not yet been discovered. Surely, then, Nessie and Bigfoot could still be out there? It's unlikely. Most newly discovered species are small, closely related to other already known species, or live in locations that are hard to get to, like the bottom of the ocean. It is extremely unlikely that an enormous species such as the Loch Ness monster or Bigfoot could live so close to humans and evade so many attempts at their discovery.

Proof

Okay, but you can't PROVE that Bigfoot doesn't exist, right?

It doesn't really work that way. To start with, it's the job of the person making a claim to prove their idea. It's not everyone else's job to prove them wrong. I can't prove that the centre of the Earth is not inhabited by miniature lava goblins, but that doesn't mean I have to take you seriously if you claim that it is.

Also, science isn't about 'proof', it's about evidence. For Nessie and Bigfoot, there is far stronger evidence that they do not exist than there is that they do. Sure, new evidence might appear one day to change this, but until then, it's best to base our understanding of the world on where the evidence is strongest.

Bioluminescence

Many life forms are able to light up the dark by using a chemical reaction to produce a glow.

Glow-worm

Tiny but sparkling, it uses its glow to attract small insects, which it then traps in silk snares a bit like a spider's web.

Will-o'-the-wisp

This glowing light lures unsuspecting prey into bogs or ponds.

Anglerfish

The bioluminescent lure that protrudes from its head looks like an angler's fishing rod, giving this deep-sea dweller its name.

Sea sparkle

This strange phenomenon turns the ocean red during the day but electric blue at night.

Foxfire

Drab by day, at night it causes rotting wood to light up like the embers of a glowing green fire.

Foxfire is caused by bioluminescent fungus growing on damp, rotting wood. In daylight, the fungus is difficult to see, and the wood looks quite ordinary. But on a dark night, the fungus glows neon green, giving it the name foxfire or 'false' fire from the French word *faux* meaning false.

The deep-sea **anglerfish** lives deep in the ocean, where no light penetrates. To attract prey, female anglerfish use a bioluminescent lure that extends from their heads like a fishing rod. Male anglerfish take a different approach. Instead of eating, males attach themselves to a female with their teeth. Over time, their bodies merge. The male receives nutrients while the female has a mate to hand whenever she wants to reproduce.

DID YOU KNOW?

Some bioluminescent animals don't produce their own glow. Instead, they play host to bacteria that do the glowing for them.

REAL

Will-o'-the-wisps and Min-Min lights, *feu follet* and *luz mala*. Many cultures have stories of strange lights hovering in midair, particularly around bogs and marshes. In England, these lights are said to be carried by mischievous spirits to lure unsuspecting travellers away from the safe path. Although these spirits are only folktales, some scientists think that burning marsh gases could be a natural explanation for the spooky floating light.

UNREAL

A dinoflagellate is a single-celled organism that is neither an animal nor a plant. When nutrients wash into the oceans after rain, dinoflagellates grow in huge numbers, creating an electric blue **'sea sparkle'** effect at night. They don't glow constantly, but flash short, intense bursts of light when the water is disturbed. At night, the result is a black ocean with sparkling blue waves crashing to the shore and glowing trails marking the passage of ships and sea creatures.

The **glow-worm** isn't really a worm, but the immature stage of a small fly called a fungus gnat. It uses its glow to attract small insects to its snares – dangling threads of silk made sticky with mucus. After 9 to 11 months as a grub, glow-worms metamorphose into adult fungus gnats. As an adult, the gnat lives only a few days. It has no mouth for eating, but simply reproduces then dies.

REAL

Among the Branches

Trees are not just for birds. Many weird and wonderful animals make their homes there.

Tarsier

With eyes so big they aren't able to move in their sockets, the tarsier looks around by turning its head up to 180 degrees in each direction.

Drop bear
Related to the koala, but much larger, it hunts its prey by dropping on it from trees.

Tree kangaroo
Its better-known cousins spend their lives on the ground, but this kangaroo lives in the trees of northern Australia and New Guinea.

Proboscis monkey
Who's this handsome fellow? Scientists believe that his enormous nose helps him to attract a mate.

Aye-aye
It's not well loved on its home island of Madagascar, perhaps due to the skeletal fingers, big ears and wide eyes that give it a spooky appearance.

REAL

The **aye-aye** uses its extremely long, thin middle finger to hunt for insect larvae... and sometimes to pick its nose (yes, really!). It taps along branches while listening closely with its bat-like ears. When it hears a grub, it gnaws an opening in the wood and catches its prey with its long finger. In Madagascan folklore, the aye-aye has traditionally been seen as an omen of death, causing some locals to kill it on sight. Today it is a protected species.

The **proboscis monkey** is named for its enormous nose, but this is not its only unusual adaptation. It has webbed feet for swimming, and its protruding belly contains a complex gut system that allows it to digest its leafy diet. As for its nose, scientists believe it serves to amplify its call to impress females and scare off rivals. Only the male monkey sports this impressive appendage, although the female's upturned nose is also quite distinctive.

REAL

UNREAL

Australians love to have a laugh... and sometimes to laugh at others. Many unsuspecting travellers to Australia have been warned about the **drop bear**, a predatory marsupial who specialises in dropping on bushwalkers from above. Locals often encourage tourists to spread Vegemite on their bodies or wear forks in their hair to ward off the legendary creature's attack.

REAL

The tiny **tarsier** is less than 15 centimetres long, but has truly enormous eyes for its body size. While most nocturnal animals have a reflective layer at the back of their eye that allows them to make the most of the small amount of light available at night, the tarsier does not. Instead, it has evolved eyes that are as large as its brain – sometimes larger – and so big that they cannot move in their sockets.

Yes! Some kangaroos really do live in trees. Found only in New Guinea and Far North Queensland, the **tree kangaroo** is well adapted to life in the branches, with shorter hind legs than its ground-dwelling cousins, but stronger front legs for climbing. It is also an excellent jumper. It can jump up to 9 metres from tree to tree and can even jump to the ground from heights of up to 18 metres. That's around the height of a five-storey building!

REAL

Healing Powers

Each of these creatures has amazing abilities that allow them to heal themselves of serious injuries, or even to live their lives all over again.

Immortal jellyfish

When sick, old or injured, it can revert to a younger version of itself and live its life again.

Planarian

Some types of planarian tear themselves in half as a way of reproducing.

Axolotl

This amphibian can regrow limbs and heal its organs of injuries that would kill most animals.

Sea cucumber

When threatened, it shoots its innards out its anus to buy itself time to escape. The missing organs grow back later.

Hydra

If its head is removed, this Greek sea-snake grows back not one but two replacements! It can repeat this multiple times, leaving it with many heads.

33

Unlike its vegetable namesake, the **sea cucumber** is not a plant but a primitive animal without eyes or a brain. Though neither fast nor fierce, it is not completely defenceless when faced with a predator. If it feels threatened, the sea cucumber can eject its digestive organs out of its mouth or its anus, and simply grow them back later thanks to its impressive regenerative abilities.

The **axolotl** is a curious creature indeed. While most amphibians undergo metamorphosis as they grow – such as when a tadpole turns into a frog – an axolotl never really grows up. Although it develops lungs, the axolotl lives its entire life in the water, keeping its feathery gills. It also has the most impressive healing powers of any vertebrate. It is able to heal or regrow limbs, heart, spinal cord and even its brain!

In Greek mythology, the hero Heracles was sent to kill the **hydra** by his stepmother, Hera, as part of a cruel plot. Hera believed that Heracles had no hope of killing the monster, which grew back two heads in place of each one that was cut off. But Hera underestimated her stepson, who realised that a flaming torch held to the bloody neck would stop the heads from regrowing and allow him to defeat the beast.

A **planarian** can regrow its entire body from the tiniest of parts. Its tail, if separated from its head, can swim through the water immediately, although, without a mouth, it can't eat. This tail will grow eyes, mouth and other missing body parts, until it looks like a much smaller replica of the original animal. To complete the strangeness, a planarian that regrows from only a tail keeps the memories it had before it lost its head!

REAL

The lifecycle of a jellyfish consists of several stages: egg, larva, polyp and finally medusa, the adult form that most people are familiar with. If the **immortal jellyfish** is in danger, it can transform itself from medusa back to the earlier polyp phase. When the threat has passed, this polyp will create buds that will eventually be released to grow into adult jellyfish that are genetically identical to the original animal.

REAL

De-livered

In Greek mythology, the god Prometheus was sentenced by Zeus to be tied to a rock and have his liver eaten by an eagle every day. Each night the liver grew back before being eaten again the following day. The human liver really does have the power to regrow after a part of it is removed, but it's not clear whether the ancient Greeks, thousands of years ago, knew this.

35

A Fish Out of Water

A fish lives in water, doesn't it? Not always! Some creatures live in quite unexpected environments.

① Diving bell spider

Like humans, spiders need air to survive. So how does this spider manage to live most of its life under water, even sleeping and laying eggs beneath the surface?

② Sewer alligators

Don't look down! Usually found in the USA's warm southeast, one resourceful group of alligators has made its home in the sewers of New York City.

③ Mangrove killifish

It's a literal fish out of water – at least some of the time. Unlike most fish, the mangrove killifish is able to survive more than 2 months on land!

❹ Hanging snakes

In a cave near the village of Kantemó in Mexico, snakes hang from the rocky ceiling to snatch bats from midair as they fly out into the night.

❺ Goats in trees

Visit Morocco in the right season and you will find flocks of goats high in the argan trees, munching on their fruit.

According to legend, New York is swarming with so many enormous **sewer alligators** that sewer workers need shotguns on the job. This story does have a small grain of truth to it. Young alligators, likely abandoned pets, are sometimes found in the ponds, parks and sewers of New York. They are generally small, and scientists say that the New York climate is much too cold for an adult alligator to survive long.

UNREAL

The **mangrove killifish** lives in pools, ditches and muddy areas of mangrove forests that dry up for parts of the year. For most fish this would pose a serious problem, but not for the mangrove killifish. It can survive in moist leaves, abandoned crab burrows or hollow logs for up to 2 months, breathing through its skin.

REAL

It's a vision to send a chill down your spine: a great cloud of bats flapping their way into the night while **hanging snakes** snatch them from the air. With so many bats, most of them get away. But for the snakes, it's like having their nightly meal delivered straight to their door... or rather, their jaw.

REAL

38

The **diving bell spider** lives life in a bubble, quite literally. To survive under water, the spider builds a silken web canopy between reeds or other water plants and fills the area beneath with air, creating a bubble – or diving bell – that allows it to breathe freely in its watery home. The spider transports air from the surface by trapping it in the small hairs around its abdomen.

DID YOU KNOW?

If you push an upturned cup straight down into a sink full of water, a pocket of air is trapped inside. A diving bell is a much larger version of this concept that allows humans to explore the underwater world.

REAL

At first glance, **goats**, with their spindly legs, hooves and stumpy tails, might seem completely unsuited to climbing. But these creatures are some of the world's greatest mountaineers, and they're not afraid to try out their skills in trees, tempted there by delicious fruit. Sadly, the goats have become so popular a sight in Morocco that farmers have been known to lift unwilling animals into the trees and even tether them there to attract tourists.

REAL

Plants and Fungi

Think plants are boring? Think again! Plants and fungi can be just as wild and wacky as their animal counterparts.

CARNIVOROUS PLANTS

SPAGHETTI TREE

Carnivorous plants

While most plants get their nutrients from the ground through their roots, these species add to their diet by consuming insects, spiders and sometimes even mice. Yum!

Spaghetti tree

Did you know that spaghetti is grown on a tree? It's a valuable commercial crop in Italy and southern Switzerland.

Sandbox tree

This prickly plant doesn't want to be friends. It has poisonous sap, sharp spines and exploding fruit capable of causing serious injury.

Zombie-ant fungus

This parasite uses mind control on the ants it infects before consuming them from the inside. Yikes!

Telegraph plant

Native to Asia, this pea plant dances to the sound of music.

SANDBOX TREE

TELEGRAPH PLANT

ZOMBIE-ANT FUNGUS

41

Many plants can move. Vines wrap themselves around trees, and some flowers turn towards the sun as it moves across the sky. But it's unusual for a plant to move fast enough to be seen with the naked eye. The **telegraph plant** is one such plant. For each full-sized leaf, the plant has two small leaflets that move quickly in response to light and sound. Why do they do this? Nobody knows.

REAL

UNREAL

Spaghetti is made from flour and water, which is rolled into a dough and cut into thin strips before being dried. But on 1 April 1957, British television station the BBC broadcast a false news report about the bumper spaghetti crop in Switzerland as an April Fool's joke. The next day, hundreds of people called the BBC wanting to know where they could get their very own **spaghetti tree**.

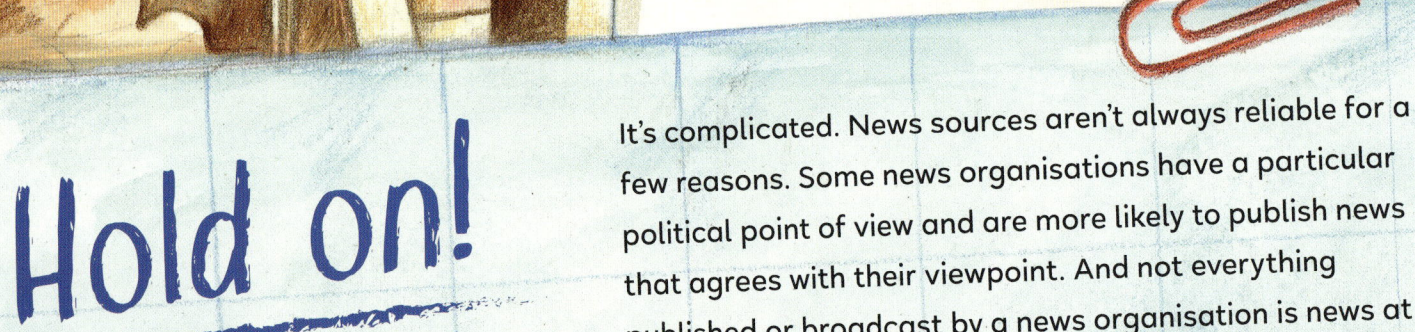

Hold on!

The BBC is the UK's national broadcaster and a well-respected news organisation. Shouldn't that be a reliable source of information?

It's complicated. News sources aren't always reliable for a few reasons. Some news organisations have a particular political point of view and are more likely to publish news that agrees with their viewpoint. And not everything published or broadcast by a news organisation is news at all. It may be paid advertising or an opinion piece trying to convince you of something. News media can also simply be wrong, particularly with news that is just breaking or changing fast. And of course, on the first day of April, it pays to be sceptical of all information, wherever it comes from.

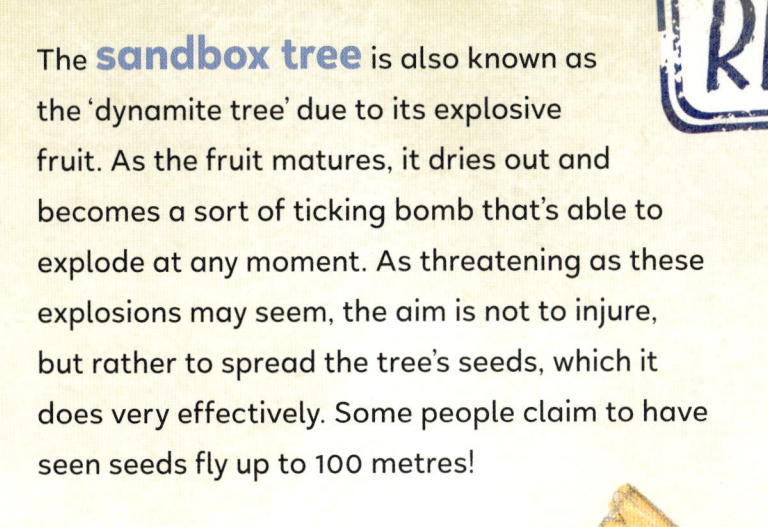

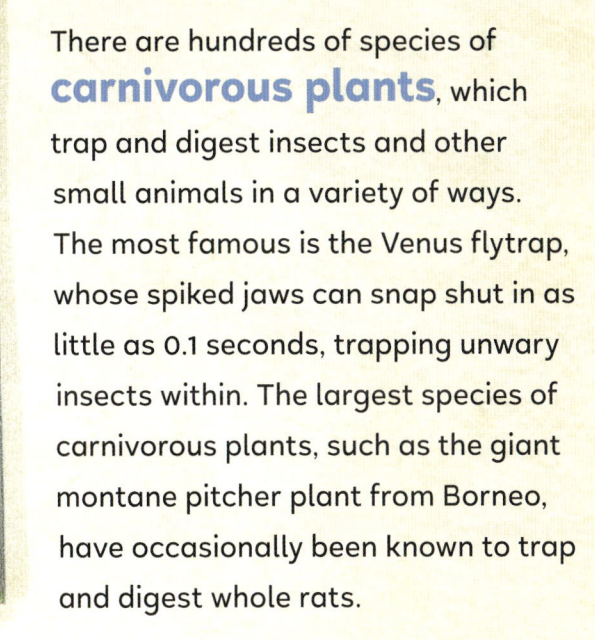

The **sandbox tree** is also known as the 'dynamite tree' due to its explosive fruit. As the fruit matures, it dries out and becomes a sort of ticking bomb that's able to explode at any moment. As threatening as these explosions may seem, the aim is not to injure, but rather to spread the tree's seeds, which it does very effectively. Some people claim to have seen seeds fly up to 100 metres!

REAL

REAL

There are hundreds of species of **carnivorous plants**, which trap and digest insects and other small animals in a variety of ways. The most famous is the Venus flytrap, whose spiked jaws can snap shut in as little as 0.1 seconds, trapping unwary insects within. The largest species of carnivorous plants, such as the giant montane pitcher plant from Borneo, have occasionally been known to trap and digest whole rats.

REAL

It's a terrifying prospect... if you're an ant. The **zombie-ant fungus** takes over not just its host's body, but also its mind. An infected ant is compelled to find a location with just the right conditions for the fungus to grow. There the ant stays, never moving while the fungus grows inside it, eventually bursting from the base of the ant's head, ready to spread its tiny spores to the ant's brothers and sisters.

43

Hoaxes and Jokesters

History contains many tales of hoaxes created as jokes and pranks, or by people seeking fame or money.

The Cottingley Fairies

Cousins Elsie Wright and Frances Griffiths were only children when they photographed themselves with fairies by a small stream near their home. When the photos became public, they quickly spread to newspapers around the world. Only when Elsie and Frances were old women did they admit that the photos had been a practical joke that got out of hand. The 'fairies' were hand-drawn pictures held up with hatpins.

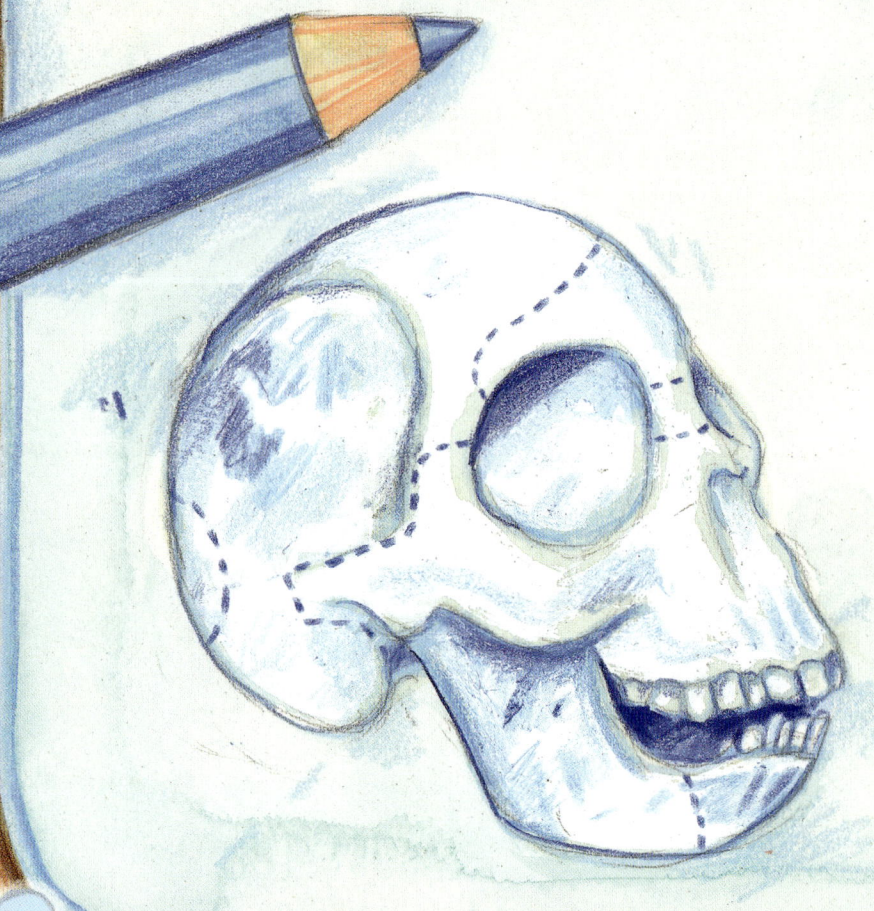

The Piltdown Man

In 1912, amateur archaeologist Charles Dawson claimed to have discovered the bones of an ancient species partway between modern humans and prehistoric apes. It was a thrilling discovery that was described as the 'missing link' in the evolution from apes to humans. It wasn't until decades later that scientists were able to prove the Piltdown Man was actually a mix of a human skull, an orangutan jaw and chimpanzee teeth filed down to make them look human.

The Pacific Northwest tree octopus

While Charles Dawson must have put a lot of effort into making his fraudulent Piltdown Man, all the creator of the Pacific Northwest tree octopus needed to do was to build a website. The supposedly endangered tree octopus was created as a joke in 1998 and has since been used to show just how easy it is to be tricked by information you find on the internet.

Show me the money

Famed 19th-century showman P.T. Barnum was known for taking a flexible approach to the truth, particularly where there was money to be made. His museum in New York City cost 25 cents for admission and featured a 'mermaid' specimen made from the tail of a fish sewn to the head and torso of a monkey. Though not many advertisers these days are quite so brazen, it is worth casting a sceptical eye over any 'facts' presented by someone wanting to sell you something.

Animal Mash-ups

These animals seem like strange mash-ups of more familiar creatures, with quite unexpected results.

Platypus
Duck meets beaver in this unique, egg-laying mammal.

Jerboa
Is it a mouse or a miniature kangaroo?

Shug monkey

This English sheep dog gets its name from its monkey-like face.

Mangalica pig

Its white, curly coat makes it a pig in sheep's clothing.

Flying fish

Is it a bird? Is it a plane? No, it's a fish that flies, of course.

A fish with wings? Surely not. Strictly speaking, the 'wings' on a **flying fish** are pairs of fins and its flying is technically gliding. All the same, for a fish to travel up to 200 metres through the air using its own momentum is an impressive feat. The flying fish uses its gliding skills to escape predators. It builds up speed beneath the surface before launching itself into the air, where it can reach speeds of over 70 kilometres per hour.

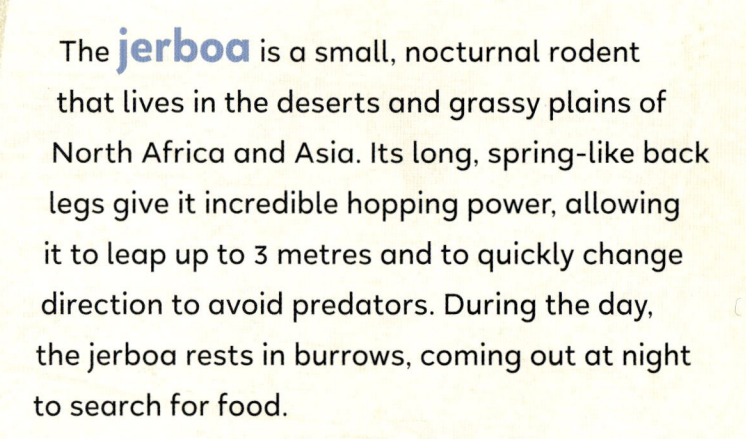

REAL

REAL

The **jerboa** is a small, nocturnal rodent that lives in the deserts and grassy plains of North Africa and Asia. Its long, spring-like back legs give it incredible hopping power, allowing it to leap up to 3 metres and to quickly change direction to avoid predators. During the day, the jerboa rests in burrows, coming out at night to search for food.

The **shug monkey** is a ghostly black dog with the face of a monkey said to have haunted Slough Hill Lane in Cambridgeshire, England. Supernatural black dogs are common in British folklore. Often they are seen as an omen of death, but some black dogs guide and protect the people they encounter. There are even stories of a living dog being killed and buried in the local churchyard so that its ghost could serve as the church's protector.

UNREAL

48

REAL

The **platypus** – a venomous, egg-laying mammal with webbed feet and a duck-like bill – is a curious creature indeed. Its evolution split from most mammals over 150 million years ago, when mammals were more closely related to reptiles. While most mammals shed their reptilian traits as they evolved, the platypus kept its egg-laying ways and is now one of only two types of egg-laying mammals in the world.

Unconscious bias

People tend to unconsciously seek out information that agrees with what they already know, believe or value, and reject information that doesn't. When British scientists were first sent a platypus specimen in the late 1700s, it was so different from the animals they had seen before that many thought it must be a hoax.

REAL

The luxuriant curly locks of the **Mangalica pig** are enough to make anyone look twice. Its winter coat is so thick and curly that it would not look out of place in a sheep pen. Mangalica pigs were first bred in Hungary in the 1830s, but lost popularity in the middle of the 20th century. The breed almost died out until, in 1991, a Spanish businessman looking to make the perfect ham began a breeding program that brought the Mangalica back from the brink.

49

Extreme Habitats

Would you be able to survive in water that is close to boiling? Could you live without oxygen? Discover animals that can survive in the most extreme circumstances.

Salamander

This amphibian likes it hot! It is resistant to fire and able to pass through flames completely unharmed.

Tardigrade

A true survivor, it can withstand some of the most extreme conditions of any animal, including the vacuum of space.

WOOD FROG

DUMBO OCTOPUS

Wood frog

Icy winters freeze it almost solid for several months of the year, but in the spring, this frog thaws out and continues its life.

Dumbo octopus

Deep in the ocean, the pressure is enough to crush a car, but this is just one of many species living far beneath the surface.

Pompeii worm

Discovered in the 1980s, it lives in and around hydrothermal vents at the bottom of the ocean where molten rock, or magma, heats the water to very high temperatures.

POMPEII WORM

REAL

Tiny **tardigrades**, also known as water bears, are less than 1 millimetre long. But don't let their size fool you – these critters are tough! They can survive extreme conditions including high pressure, dehydration and temperatures as low as -270°C and as high as 150°C. Scientists have even tested their survival in space. Although many survived the airless environment, solar radiation proved too much for even these otherwise indestructible invertebrates.

In North America, winter temperatures can drop below -40°C. While some animals migrate south or hibernate in caves, the **wood frog** has a different strategy. As the temperature drops, its body freezes. It stops breathing and its heart stops beating. For most animals, this would mean certain death. But the wood frog fills its cells with a sugary syrup that protects them during the deep freeze. In spring, the frog defrosts, completely unharmed by its experience.

REAL

UNREAL

The **salamander** is real, but its ability to withstand fire is entirely mythical. Like frogs, salamanders are amphibians who generally remain near water their entire lives. So where did the stories of their resistance to fire come from? Salamanders like to hide in hollow logs. When these were collected for firewood and thrown onto the flames, the frightened salamander would dart out, giving people the idea that they had appeared out of the flames themselves.

The water emitted by hydrothermal vents is hot, acidic and so thick with particles and chemicals it looks like plumes of smoke. Yet some life forms seem to thrive in these hostile conditions. The **Pompeii worm** makes its home in tubes built directly on the hot vent chimneys. A layer of bacteria on its body may help to protect it from the extreme heat, while its movements mix cooler ocean water with the heated water in the tubes.

The **dumbo octopus** takes its name from Disney's flying cartoon elephant. Like the cartoon Dumbo, who uses over-large ears to fly, the dumbo octopus moves through the water by flapping large, ear-like fins on either side of its head. It lives deep in the ocean, where the pressure is around 300 to 500 times the pressure on land. These extreme pressures would crush a human to death, but the dumbo octopus cannot survive without them.

Remarkable Reptiles

Reptiles suffer from something of a bad reputation among humans, who will often run screaming at the sight of a snake, crocodile or even a lizard. But take a closer look and you'll find some truly fascinating creatures.

❶ Horned lizard

It may not be the most effective defence around, but it is among the most unusual. The horned lizard squirts blood almost a metre from its eyes to repel predators.

❷ Hoop snake

You'll need to be fast to outrun this snake! To gain speed, it clasps its tail in its mouth and rolls downhill in the form of a hoop.

❸ Chameleon

This lizard has a bigger bag of tricks than most. It changes colour, moves its eyes in two directions at once and whips out its tongue with more than 250 times gravitational acceleration.

❹ Komodo dragon

It's the largest lizard in the world, weighing up to 140 kilograms and measuring 3 metres long.

❺ Green basilisk lizard

Would you like to be able to run on water without sinking? This reptile can, and its seemingly miraculous ability has earned it the nickname the 'Jesus Christ lizard'.

REAL

Despite its name, the **komodo dragon** neither flies nor breathes fire. It is, however, the world's largest living lizard and is capable of killing pigs, deer and even water buffalo with its venomous bite. Komodo dragon venom prevents the blood of its prey from clotting, causing them to become weak or even die due to blood loss. Some scientists also think that bacteria living in the komodo dragon's mouth contribute to the death of its prey.

REAL

The **green basilisk lizard** shares its name with the mythical basilisk of ancient legend. In mythology, the basilisk is said to be able to kill with a single glance. The real green basilisk lizard isn't quite so extraordinary, but it is known for a pretty neat trick. If threatened, this lizard can run on water thanks to scaly fringes on its toes that give its hind feet a large surface area.

REAL

The **horned lizard** has a wide body and a blunt face so toad-like that it is often called the horned toad. Its preferred approach to self-defence is simply to blend into its surroundings, but if this fails, it turns to more interesting options. By inflating itself to twice its size, the lizard becomes a spiky balloon. It can even spurt blood at an attacker by bursting tiny blood vessels around its eyes.

Many people think that a **chameleon** can copy any pattern in its surroundings in order to blend in. This is not the case. Although its natural green and brown colouring does help it to blend in with its environment, the chameleon uses its most colourful displays for communication. Aggressive males will display bright colours during a fight, while females use dark colours to show that they aren't interested in a mate.

REAL

The **hoop snake** is a North American legend that has been told for hundreds of years. Stories tell of a snake that chases its quarry by rolling like a hoop before striking with a venomous 'horn' in its tail. According to legend, the snake's horn is so venomous that if it strikes a tree, the tree will die within 24 hours. Rewards offered for evidence of such a snake have never been successfully claimed.

UNREAL

It Was THIS Big!

Have you ever heard a fisher's tale of the giant fish that got away? Or a scary story about an enormous snake, spider, bat or rat? Humans love to exaggerate, but the size of some creatures really is extraordinary.

Japanese spider crab

Like a giant, deep-sea daddy-long-legs, its 30-centimetre body is surrounded by spindly legs that give it a span of up to 4 metres across.

Amazonian giant centipede

It grows up to 30 centimetres long – that's the length of a standard school ruler!

Congolese giant spider

Truly the stuff of nightmares, this arachnid measures up to 1 metre across.

Flemish giant rabbit

Much bigger than your average cottontail, this giant can weigh as much as a human toddler and measure well over a metre long.

Giant Gippsland earthworm

This Australian native can grow up to 2 metres long and 2 centimetres in diameter, although most will only grow to about 1 metre in length.

Many people claim to have seen the **Congolese giant spider** – known locally as *j'ba fofi* – but no strong evidence of its existence has ever been found. According to local legend, the *j'ba fofi* spins almost invisible webs at ground level to capture birds, small animals and sometimes even humans. Enormous arachnids have been reported all over the world, but the largest scientifically verified spider is the goliath bird-eater, which is about the size of a medium pizza.

UNREAL

REAL

The **Flemish giant rabbit** was first bred for its fur and meat hundreds of years ago. Rabbit stew isn't so popular these days, so Flemish giants are usually kept as pets or bred as show animals. When fully grown, they commonly weigh around 9 kilograms – about 3 times as much as other rabbit breeds. If keeping one as a pet appeals to you, keep in mind that their appetite is as large as they are!

REAL

Few people have ever seen a **giant Gippsland earthworm**. They live only in a small area east of Melbourne and are rarely seen above ground. Local farmers know they are there because they can hear the squelching, gurgling noise they make as they move through their moist underground burrows. These creatures are giants from the get-go, measuring around 18 centimetres at birth and typically growing to 80–100 centimetres long.

REAL

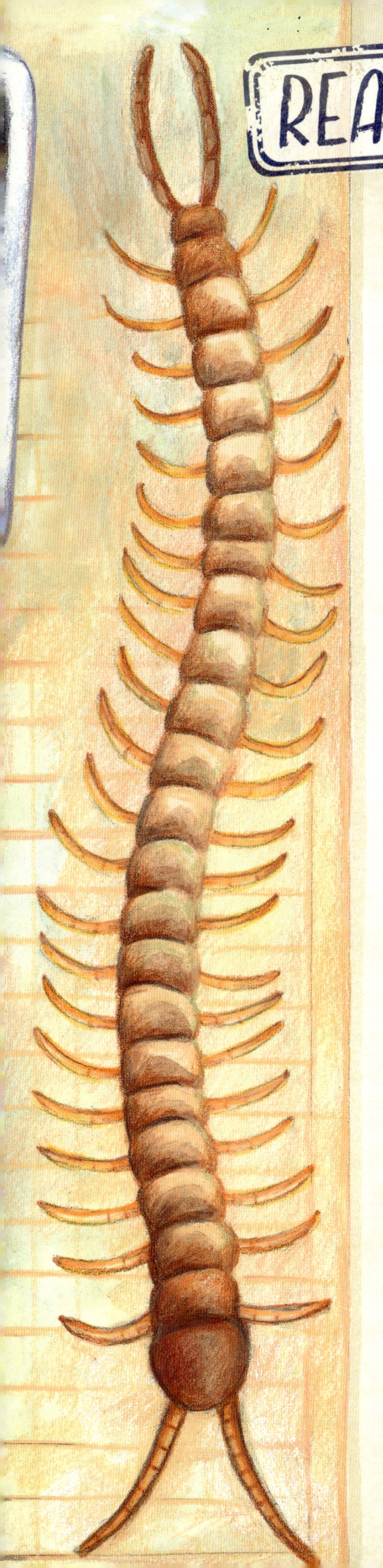

The **Amazonian giant centipede** stalks the rainforests of South America, hunting for spiders, snakes, scorpions and small mammals. It's not afraid to take on animals larger than itself...for good reason. In addition to dozens of legs, the Amazonian giant centipede has two claw-like forcipules near its head that it uses to inject venom into its prey. Watch out! The venom is rarely fatal to humans, but it will give you a nasty sting.

REAL

Although it will grow to be a giant, when born, the **Japanese spider crab** only measures around 1 millimetre across. As it grows, the crab will moult – or shed its shell – many times, each time growing a new, larger shell to replace the one it has cast off. The crab's body stops growing when it reaches adulthood, but its legs continue, helping it to reach its enormous size.

61

We did it!

Thanks for helping me return our legendary creatures to where they belong. Were you surprised by what we found? If you had trouble separating real from unreal, you're not alone. Life on Earth is pretty extraordinary. It can be hard to believe some real-life animals and plants actually exist.

As for our myths and legends, don't be fooled into thinking that unreal means unimportant. Before modern science, myths were a way for people to explain what they saw in the world around them. Myths also helped people share their values and talk about right and wrong. Even today, fiction is a way for storytellers all across the globe to talk about what it means to be human. So yes, myths *are* unreal, but I think they're also pretty cool. Don't you?

63

Index

A

Amazonian giant centipede 58, 61
anglerfish 25–26
axolotl 33–34
aye-aye 29–30

B

Barnum, P.T. 45
Bigfoot 23
bioluminescence 24–27

C

carnivorous plant 40, 43
chameleon 55, 57
chupacabra 10, 13
Congolese giant spider 59–60
Cottingley Fairies, the 44

D

deep-sea creature 6–7, 9, 25–26, 51, 53
defensive behaviour 9, 33–34, 48, 54, 56
dinoflagellates 25, 27
diprotodon 15, 17
diving bell spider 36, 39
drop bear 29–30
dumbo octopus 51, 53

E

endangered species 11, 12, 30
evidence 3, 22–23

F

Flemish giant rabbit 59–60
flying fish 47–48
foxfire 25–26
fungus 26, 41, 43
funnel-web spider 19–20

G

giant Gippsland earthworm 59–60
giant squid 9
glow-worm 24, 27
goat in tree 37, 39
green basilisk lizard 55–56
grey nurse shark 11–12
ground sloth 14, 17

H

horned lizard 54, 56
hydra 33–34

I

immortal jellyfish 32, 35

J

Japanese spider crab 58, 61
jerboa 46, 48

K

komodo dragon 55–56
kraken 6, 9

L

lamprey 6, 8
Loch Ness monster 22

M

Mangalica pig 47, 49
mangrove killifish 36, 38
marine iguana 6, 8
mating behaviour 13, 26, 30, 57
megafauna 14–17
megalodon 14, 16
metamorphosis 20, 27, 34
moa 15–16
Mongolian death worm 18, 21
murder hornet *see northern giant hornet*

N

naked mole-rat 19, 21
narwhal 6, 8
northern giant hornet 11, 13

P

Pacific Northwest tree octopus 45
Piltdown Man, the 44
planarian 32, 35
platypus 46, 49
Pompeii worm 51, 53
predatory behaviour 6, 8, 10–13, 20, 37–38, 40–41, 43, 56
proboscis monkey 29–30
proof 23; *also see evidence*

R

reproduction 8, 26, 32
roc 15, 17

S

salamander 50, 52
sandbox tree 41, 43
sasquatch *see Bigfoot*
sea cucumber 33–34
sea sparkle 25, 27
sewer alligator 36, 38
sexual selection 30, 57
shug monkey 47–48
snake 33–34, 37–38, 55, 57
spaghetti tree 41–42
star-nosed mole 18, 20

T

tardigrade 50, 52
tarsier 28, 31
Tasmanian devil 10, 12
telegraph plant 41–42
tree kangaroo 29, 31
turtle frog 19–20

V

vampire squid 6, 9
venom 19–20, 49, 56, 57, 61

W

werewolf v
will-o'-the-wisp 24, 27
wolverine 10, 13
wood frog 51–52

Z

zombie-ant fungus 41, 43

UNREAL

Werewolves are shapeshifters: people who can transform from human form to wolf. During the 15th, 16th and 17th centuries, the general belief in these shapeshifters was so strong in some parts of Europe that people were tried and executed for the crime of being a werewolf. People today know better, and understand that werewolves only exist in stories... right?